MW01243773

LOYALTY

B.G. Meyers

(2023)

Loyalty

B.G. Meyers

Copyright © 103 Publishing Group 2023

LOYALTY

No parts of this material should be used or reproduced
without permission from the author or publisher.
Advertisements & promotion is deemed acceptable as long
as it accurately represents the brand.

All rights reserved.

ISBN: 9798376799215

CONTENTS

ACKNOWLEDGMENTS

To all the people they said would never make it. I'm living proof that you can turn your life around. Through hard work & dedication you can make dreams come true!! Never give up, and never abandon your dreams.

CHAPTER 1.
L O Y A L T Y

"We just slid on Poppo, and his top soldiers are ready to convert to working for us?" Ghost announced proudly.

"We ain't fuckin' wit dem niggas." I responded nonchalantly.

"Why not?"

"Because they ain't loyal. Think about it Ghost, they were just ridin' for Poppo. Now they're ready to get money with us."

Poppo had been my opposition in the streets for years. No matter how much I tried to compromise with him, he couldn't see pass me being a WOMAN dominating in a man's world!

"That's the game Loyalty! Ain't no real love, it's all about benefits. How can you benefit me?"

"Exactly. I'm not feedin' no strays my nigga. They gotta find their own way or starve!" I replied full of anger.

The streets had been a gift & a curse to me. I had made a lot of money in the drug trade, but I had also lost a lot of close friends. My biggest loss came at the beginning of my wave, and I had never healed from it.

"Whatever you say, I'm wit it. We've been down since day one, and nothing but death will separate me from you!!" Ghost said with all the emotions his cold soul could muster.

Sean Johnson aka "Ghost" had been my hitta since high school, and he had never once faltered in the face of danger. Most people thought we were romantically involved, but the truth was, we had never ever crossed any lines. Our friendship was strictly platonic. It was one of the strongest loves I had ever experienced in my life.

I had grown up in the city of Richmond. At 35 years old, I

had conquered the drug game. Born Lana Jackson, I was raised by my godmother Alexis Hayes. My pretty face & curvaceous 5'3" frame made me one of the baddest bitches in the city!

"Awwww, ain't you sweet!" I responded jokingly huggin' Ghost.

"C'mon Loyalty, you know how I am about all that public affection." Ghost fired back smiling.

I was on top of my game, and money was coming in by the boatload! I had soldiers puttin' on for da "Trap Stars" all through the city. I had a plug from San Diego California name "Monster," and he was in-love with my ambitious spirit. With the lowest prices on the streets, it was easy for me to fuck the game up!! Plus, my deceased boyfriend "Gunna" had given me the blueprint. Pillow talk with Gunna was about money moves, and I soaked up every drop of it. I never expected Gunna to be murdered in coldblood coming out of the "804 Lounge."

"What's our next move boss lady?" Ghost asked sincerely wanting to know the direction in which we were headed.

"I'm thinking about gettin' outta the game. It's so much other stuff we can do with this money."

"Like what?"

"Like start our own companies. I wanna buy a boutique." I announced wholeheartedly.

I had been into fashion since middle school, and dressing had become one of my passions over the years. I hadn't been able to focus on it before, because I had become consumed with the game. Monster was pushing tons of cocaine into Virginia through customs. Even though he had been living in Cali, he was connected all over the United States. He was the definition of a "Boss," and I had learned a lot from him during our business relationship.

It wasn't one hustla in the streets of Richmond that didn't know who "Loyalty" was, and that wasn't always a good thing. The streets were filled with snakes & rats, and reputation wasn't as important as it once was. However, I had still travelled down the road to riches & got right along the way!

"I don't know about that Loyalty. I don't know nothing about running no business. I've been a killer since I met you!"

"Yeah, but that shit doesn't define who you are. You oversee our whole operation every day, and it's no different from running a legitimate business." I told Ghost wanting him to understand his worth.

"I love you Loyalty, and I'll follow you into hell & back. Never will I forsake or betray you, but you gotta respect what I am." Ghost said with a tone of frustration.

"And what's that?"

"America's nightmare. Rich, black & don't give a fuck!!"

Ghost was the realest nigga I had ever met. It wasn't nothing on this earth he was afraid of, and I admired his courage. Even with that being said, I still wanted more for him. Something about how he lived made me nervous. I often felt like he would be killed in the streets by a nobody, and I wouldn't be able to stomach that pain.

"Just give it a chance. If it doesn't work, we can always get back to the streets." I pleaded.

"If you really wanna go legit, I'll be right beside you." Ghost replied trying to hide his fear of going legit.

"Okay."

(Snowman)

"I gave y'all niggas da blueprint, what else do you want?" I asked Boogie.

"Everybody trinna eat!" He fired back.

"You mean everybody trinna sit at the table, but only bosses are allowed!"

"We can't afford to play tight wit da gang. Especially

3

when Loyalty is blessin' niggas!" Boogie announced feeling salty.
Brian Banks aka "Boogie" came up rough, doin' licks for small checks. The streets of Mosby had molded him into a savage, and Boogie didn't mind one bit. He knew what it took to survive, and he was an expert at making power moves.

"So, you're tellin' me Poppo is lettin' her live!?" I asked in complete discuss.

Right now, I was in a tugga war with the "Trap Stars," mainly because they didn't want to abide by the rules I had set forth for the Southside. Loyalty had set the bar high, and I respected it to a certain extent. Most niggas felt like she didn't deserve her spot, because Gunna had left her in position. It was another way of looking at it though. Not just any female could have took his product & turned it into an empire, but she had done just that.

"Ain't no stoppin' shorty at this point. It's either make room for her or have her hit!" Boogie stated feeling challenged.

"Send your best shooters." I replied without a second thought.

CHAPTER 2.
SANTANA

"Girrrrrllll, you was killin' that bodysuit last night!" I told Loyalty.

"Thank you boo."

Loyalty had been my friend since the sixth grade. It was just something about her that I loved. She definitely was a bad bitch, and that motivated me to be one as well. Together we drove niggas crazy! Appearance wise, we were night & day. I was slim, thick with long flowing blonde hair, and my ass wasn't nowhere near as big as hers. I had stripped in "Daddy Rabbits" for a few months, but it ended up not being for me. I was more of a cute secretary type of bitch.

I still remember the day when Loyalty told me she was planning on hustling. I couldn't believe it! I understood the mechanics of the drug trade. It was simple, you supplied someone's demand. I had fucked a few hustlers, but I had never dreamed of selling drugs.

"I saw that nigga Grimey checkin' you out. He was all up your ass!!" Santana screamed playfully.

"He ain't my type though." Loyalty responded with an uninterested tone.

"What?! That nigga is FINE, and I heard he got da best head in Richmond!"

"Girrrrlll, who told you that?" Loyalty asked me laughingly.

"I don't remember." I lied.

Truth be told, I just wanted my friend to be happy. I watched as Gunna's death tore her apart. I thought she would never bounce back, but somehow, she did.

"I'm thinkin' about buying a boutique. Going legit.

5

Gettin' us outta these streets." Loyalty blurted out.

"What does Ghost think?"

"He's trinna wrap his head around it, but he's being open minded. These streets don't love us Santana, and you know I'm right. Why are we still trinna squeeze juice from a turnip?!"

"I'm not trippin'. I saved a few dollars from our last move, so I can invest." I offered sincerely.

"Let's find a space, then we can talk investments."

"Cool."

(Ghost)

"Every time we cross paths, you're always on me." Brooklyn said seductively.

"Because I'm feelin' you!" I replied confidently.

"You don't even know me." She fired back.

"Well, we can change all that."

Brooklyn was drop dead gorgeous, and we always seemed to mingle in the same places. The last time we were in "Ma Michelle's," she recited a poem for open mic night. Her words & body movements mixed had me hypnotized, and I found myself really wanting to get to know her.

"What do you want with a girl like me Ghost?" Brooklyn questioned with wide eyes.

"Everything! I can see myself building something with you." I emphasized.

"I've done my homework on you, and your reputation isn't a good one." She announced.

"You can't believe everything you hear." I replied grabbing her hand.

She didn't seem to be alarmed by our sudden contact, and I found myself standing eye to eye with her.

"Let's just see what happens." Brooklyn said in almost a whisper.

B.G. Meyers

"I got you."

(LOYALTY)

Now that Poppo was dead, I had complete locks on the Southside. Deep down I was proud of myself for surviving as many street wars as I did, and now it was time for me to elevate my game. I wasn't trinna be 40 years old & still moving narcotics in the streets. I had been in the game for over 10 years, and I had made a fortune within that time period.

"What's up Thicky Minaj?" Roller greeted me as I approached his 560 Mercedes Benz.

"Shut up!" I replied laughing at his corny joke. Reginald Harris aka "Roller" was a big deal in the streets of Richmond. He had put in his share of work, did time, came home & got right back to the bag! He wanted to connect with me on a physical level, but I wasn't into fuckin' local dope boyz. I wanted the type of power that came from exclusivity, so I never made my pussy available for niggas in the game. Gunna was a special exception because it was just something about him that I couldn't resist. Some people thought it was his money, but I never cared about that for real.

"To what do I owe this honor?" Roller inquired as I slid into the passenger seat on his money green Benz.

"Business." I stated firmly.

"I'm listening." He replied giving me his full attention.

"Poppo is no longer with us, so I'm sure that leaves a void in your operation."

"Meaning?"

"I can match his quality for 5% less." I revealed my intentions.

"What about us?"

"Us?" I repeated.

Loyalty

B.G. Meyers

"Yeah. You know I feel about you Loyalty. I've been
trinna get wit you since back in da days."
"I told you my nigga, I'm here for business. I got da
best prices & product in town, and you're worried about a
nut! Let's get this money Roller, because all that other shit
ain't gone happen!" I fired back with a serious expression.
"When can I score?" He asked appearing to be
embarrassed.
"Today, if your money straight!" I stated getting out
of his car.

(GHOST)

"What do you think about Loyalty's plan?" Santana
asked curiously.
"I don't know what to think. All we've ever done was
trap, but I'm not mad at her for wanting more for us."
Santana placed her hand on my thigh as we sat on her
couch & talked. It wasn't long before her hand made it to my
groin, and she began to massage my manhood through my
jeans. We had been creeping around behind Loyalty's back
for the last 6 months. It wasn't serious at all. It was just
something we both needed to escape from time to time.
"I love how your dick feels in my mouth!" Santana
whispered once she had my penis free.
"I love how your mouth feels period!" I said as my
dick grew in her hand.
She began to lick the head of my penis slow, leaving it shiny
from her spit. Then she took it completely into her mouth &
began to suck lightly.
"Mmmmmm!" She groaned as she picked up the
pace.
"Damn!" I growled pumping all of my thickness into
her mouth.
She began to suck more steady, allowing more into her

8

mouth. Damn, she had the best head I'd ever had, and if Loyalty hadn't made a specific rule forbidding members from being involved,
I would probably wife Santana up!! We had a lot of things in common, and she was just an all-around good fit for me.

"You gone fuck me daddy?" She asked while strippin' off her clothes.

"Of course, I am."

CHAPTER 3.
<u>N A S A</u>

"Yo Evans, you got a legal visit. Call me when you're ready." C/O Taylor informed me.

I had been housed at Sussex 1 State Prison for the last 5 years. I went from having the streets on lock, to being treated like a piece of trash. I couldn't see myself being incarcerated for too many more years. My appeal had made it to the United Supreme Court, and my lawyer "Marie Rodriguez" was a beast when it came to post conviction cases.

"I'm ready Taylor." I yelled out of my cell door once I was dressed.

"Open 4b01." C/O Taylor instructed the control booth officer.

Once my cell door was opened, I stepped out onto the pod area. My mind was in a million different places as I walked to the interview room.

"I thought I had a legal visit." I questioned after seeing a detective seated inside the interview room.

"Sit down." Detective Martin ordered.

"What's this about?"

"Your relationship with Lana Jackson."

"Who?"

"Oh. I guess you only know her as Loyalty!" The detective stated.

"I don't got nothing to say."

"It's indictment season. Do you think she'd take a case for you? Let me answer that, HELL NO!! But you're willing to rot in here for her."

"Are you finished? Because I'm ready to go back to my cell now." I assisted.

Loyalty

B.G. Meyers

"Before you go, think about never seeing your son again. You're serving a 35-year bid, and I can have that reduced."
Detective Martin said.
    "For what?"
    "Information."
    "What kind of information?" I asked curiously.
    "Who killed Gregory Bateman?" The Detective questioned staring directly at me.

    Once I was back in my cell, I couldn't stop thinking about what the detective had asked me. Gunna was the top dog in Richmond before someone shot him in front of the club one night. A lot of bodies dropped that week because Loyalty wanted revenge for her boyfriend's death. She had ordered a hit on anyone that was associated with his killing, but no one had ever taken ownership for his shooting. Now the police wanted to implicate Loyalty, saying that she had him killed for his money. It wasn't such a bad idea, but the streets knew she loved Gunna unconditionally. She loved him so much, that she paid his remaining debt with his plug & she carried on his Trap Stars legacy.
    "You thinkin' about snitchin' on that bitch?" Teddy asked me.
    "Fuck NO!! I ain't no rat my nigga." I lied.
Teddy had been my roommate for a couple of months, and I honestly thought something was fishy about him. None of his stories added up, and no one from the city knew him. He said he was originally from North Carolina and had gotten arrested in Richmond his first few days out here.
    "Man, you gotta think about your son. He needs you out there." Teddy reasoned.
    "If I tell on Loyalty, I'll be dead before I reach the streets!"
    "She got that much power?"
    "And more!" I confirmed.
I had never contemplated snitching before this very moment,

but I was tired of being incarcerated. Here I was serving time, while other Trap Stars were free making big moves. It wasn't fair if you asked me.

"I'm bout to use da jack right quick, I'll be back." Teddy announced walking out of the cell's door.

I had to figure out what I was gone do, because Detective Martin said I didn't have long. It was an open investigation on the Trap Stars, so their days of gettin' money were limited. I just wanted to be free again, but I wasn't sure at what cost!!

(LOYALTY)

"Who told you that?" Ghost asked.

Shit was beginning to get real in the streets, and niggas were secretly coming for my head.

"Boogie." I replied with tears in my eyes.

"It don't make sense. Why would Snowman want you dead?"

"Because he was supplying Poppo. I took food off his table, and now he wants to take me out of this world! It's okay though because I ain't going down that easy."

"I say we move on him first. Catch em off guard and take em for everything he's worth!" Ghost emphasized.

"This was supposed to be my exit Boogie. My victory lap, but instead I'm gettin' pulled deeper in." I said with a hint frustration in my voice.

I knew where killing Snowman would lead us, but it was a must-do situation. He had green lighted me to be hit, and the only logical response was for me to strike first. That's how the game is played when you're dealing with murder & lawless individuals. You have to be prepared to pull the trigger on anybody at any time!!

"It's your call Loyalty, but I really don't think we should pussy foot around on this one."

"Do it!!!!"

CHAPTER 4.
<u>ROLLER</u>

       2023 came in with a bang, and I was ready to take over the city. Get down or lay down was the motto, and my goons weren't pickin' & choosing the targets. I had earned my bones in the streets, and now it was time for me to elevate. The money had to match my ambition. Loyalty was on my list of things to do! She was playing hard to get at the moment, but all bad bitches did in the beginning.

       "When you gone take me outta town Roller?" Miami asked with an attitude.

We had been fuckin' for a couple of months, but she really wasn't fittin' the bill. Her chinky eyes & full lips reminded me of a younger version of Cardi B, and her body type also resembled hers. Miami was definitely gorgeous, but she wasn't Loyalty.

       "Where you wanna go?" I replied not caring for real.

       "To Miami. I've never been before." She announced poppin' her bubblegum as she chewed it ratchetly.

       "Why is your name Miami then?"

       "Because that's where I plan on moving to one day." She fired back.

Before I could bake her ass my phone started ringing.

       "Yoooo!" I answered.

       "It's me. I gave Ghost the rundown, now it's just a waiting game." Boogie explained.

       "What about Loyalty?" I asked concerned about her well-being.

       "She gone be good my nigga. When it's all said & done, you can have her come work for you." Boogie said laughingly.

       "And what about Ghost?"

       "Hopefully, he doesn't make it through the storm! If

so, he'll most definitely be a problem for us."
"Well, let's pray he dies in a cloud of gun smoke!"
"I'll hit you when everything is everything." Boogie
stated.
Things were really looking promising. It was a brilliant idea
for us to play Snowman & Loyalty against one another,
because if either of them died it would leave a section of the
city up for grabs. Me & Boogie wanted to supply both sides
of town with product, because that equaled more money. My
operation was boomin', but I needed to get established
outside of Jackson Ward. This was my power move on the
city, and I was unapologetically happy about it. All we had to
do was wait. One of them would surely try to eliminate the
other.
"I feel like celebrating." I told Miami once I hung the
phone up.
"What you got in mind?" She asked seductively.
Without giving her a verbal response. I zipped down my
zipper & freed myself.
"Oh, I see."

(NASA)

"You've been actin' jumpy lately. Are you okay?"
Teddy asked me.
"Yeah, I'm good! Just thinking about my son. I don't
want him to grow up without a father like I did."
"Sounds like you're considering that deal you were
offered."
"I keep tellin' you, I ain't no snitch my nigga!"
My aggression was beginning to show, because I felt as if
Teddy was trying to play me. Nobody openly admitted to
snitchin', but the part that hurt worse was the fact that I was
actually considering it. I wanted to go home and being loyal
to Loyalty wasn't gettin' me nowhere. Yeah, she had retained

me a lawyer, but that was the least she could've done. I had
sold bricks of cocaine for her in the city of Richmond!

"I'm not callin' you a rat NASA; you're buggin' right
now. I'm just sayin', is being a real nigga worth missin' out on
your son's wonder years?" Teddy reasoned.

"I did a lot for them. Moved shit & hit niggas!!" I
boasted.

"You were in da mix like that?"

"I almost ran that shit for her. The only nigga that
had more clout than me, was Ghost."

"I heard dude was a certified killa!"

"Dat nigga is heartless! I watched him kill a father &
his son one time over a bag of weed." I told him.

"Weed?"

"Yeah, WEED! The nigga shorted Ghost a few
grams & tried to talk shit. Pop, pop!! Right on the spot, not
one word was said. The son was just a causality."

"Was this on Midlothian?" Teddy asked curiously.

"Yeah."

"I remember hearing about that. They never arrested
nobody for that."

"Ghost never gets caught. That nigga is like a
phantom for real!"

"I fuck wit you NASA. I think you should take that
deal & move away from Richmond." Teddy confided in me.

"Would you?"

"Hell yeah! Loyalty don't love you bro. If she did,
your son would be good right now. Your mom would be living
comfortably. You're doing 35 years for her, and she hasn't
come to visit you once. C'mon dog, think about what I'm
saying!"

Teddy was absolutely right! I had been loyal to her &
her movement, and she hadn't done nearly enough for me.
From the drug dealin' to the random acts of violence, she
owed me more then what she was giving me. I could take
her whole empire down in one sitting with Detective Martin.
Fuck was she thinking about treating me like this?!

"You're right. I might just have to free myself!" I said with a blank look in my eyes.

(Loyalty)

"You like that?" Gunna asked as he licked down my stomach.

"Yesss, don't stop baby." I responded opening my legs, so he could continue his journey into my wetness. I felt him spread my pussy lips apart, and as soon as his tongue made contact with my clit, I couldn't hold back my moans.

"Ooooo, eat this pussy daddy, make me cum!" I closed my eyes & began to hump his face. Gunna had me open mind, body, heart & soul. I found myself wanting to be around him all day some days. I can't explain it, but it was just a certain feeling that I felt when it came to him. Ghost wasn't as fond of him, but it wasn't his decision on who I gave my heart to.

"I love you baby, looove you, ppleasee don't stop, I'm bout to cum!" I chanted as Gunna's tongue found every one of my spots.

My body began to shake uncontrollably when my orgasm started. I closed my eyes & enjoyed the different waves of pleasure I received from climaxing.

"I love you too bae." Gunna said lovingly.

He was everything I needed in a man. Intelligent, ambitious, good looking, loving & great in bed!! I always told myself I wouldn't end up with a street nigga, but he had changed my perspective on that. I watched as he positioned his self to penetrate me, and I couldn't wait to feel him inside me. Gunna really knew how to satisfy me, and my body yearned for his sex. Before we could begin our love making, I was startled by a knock at my door.
KNOCK! KNOCK! KNOCK!

Loyalty

B.G. Meyers

I sat up in my bed half sleep, realizing that I had been dreaming. Shit, I swore to myself. I got out of my bed & had to find my Gucci robe, because I usually slept naked.
KNOCK! KNOCK!!
      "I'm coming!" I yelled towards the door.
I walked to the front door still feeling a way about my dream, and I wasn't happy at the sight of a detective on the other side.
      "Who is it?"
      "It's Detective Martin." He announced eagerly.
I opened the door with a stank look on my face. I wanted him to know how unhappy I was with him showin' up at my house. Especially in the wee hours of the morning!
      "How can I help?" I asked sarcastically.
      "I'm sorry for intruding, but we might have some new information on your boyfriend's murder."
      "Really?" I responded shocked by his statement.
      "Yes. We may've found an eyewitness. I just have a couple questions for you." The detective said.
      "Okay, come in."

CHAPTER 5.
G H O S T

     A part of me knew Snowman had to be erased from the game, because he was a potential threat to our success. We had already eliminated Poppo, and that had been a long time in the making. He had gone against us from the beginning, and no type of reason had reached him. He wanted to push us outta the game, but Loyalty had outsmarted him in the end. Now it was Snowman's turn to meet his demise.

     I found my way through the dark hallway of his condo, and I could hear slow music blasting as I approached the front door. Murder was on mind & in my heart, and I knew what I had to do on sight. What was Snowman thinking trying to have Loyalty hit? He knew I was coming, and this would be our final meeting in life.

     I slipped his door lock with my switchblade & eased inside of his condo. The lights were completely off, but the music was loud enough to be heard all through the house. I retrieved my desert eagle 357 from my waistline and attempted to stay as close as I could to the walls. I had done this over a hundred times. Every time I killed someone, it felt like their spirit united with mine. I can't explain it, but the feeling of death filled the air. I was secretly looking forward to that feeling tonight. I wondered if Snowman's spirit would feel different, because he was a legend in these streets. Bryson Tiller's "Exchange" became louder as I walked up the staircase. I could hear voices & what sounded like moans in the distance. My all-black clothes & hoody made me resemble the grim reaper, and I felt like I was one with death at that very moment. Once I was outside of the bedroom door, I clearly heard a female's voice. Butterflies rumbled in my stomach, and my grip on my hammer tightened. I

B.G. Meyers

imagined Loyalty's face after hearing Snowman was dead, and that thought brought me immediate excitement. The same excitement I felt when I gunned Gunna down in front of the 804 Lounge. Loyalty was crushed when she found out he was dead, but he had to die! He wasn't good for her, and for some reason she couldn't see that. I knew she wouldn't understand, so I never revealed my secret to her. I was just there for her with all the support & love she needed!
I cracked the bedroom door slightly and peaked inside for a second.

"Damn, you're super wet Misha." Snowman told the brown skin beauty he was finger fuckin'!

"I wannnt you so bad Snow, give me that dick!" The woman responded with her head held back.
Without warning, I sprang into action. My presence in the room startled both of them, and they were like two deer stuck in some headlights.

"What da fuck?!" Snowman yelled with a look of displeasure.

"Oh, shit!!" Shorty blurted out trying to cover her breast.
I shot her first, because she was the closest to the entrance. Her head exploded from the impact of the bullet, and complete silence followed. As I readjusted my aim to Snowman, he said...

"I knew you would come for me, but I didn't think it would be so soon! At least look me in my eyes before you step on me."
It wasn't an unreasonable request, because there would be no witnesses to his murder. I quickly rolled my mask up & looked him in the eyes.

"You're loyal, but she's gonna be your downfall one day." Snowman announced.

"So be it!"
BOOM! BOOM! BOOM!

(Boogie)

19

Loyalty

B.G. Meyers

Money had become my underlined motivation, and the streets of Richmond was my new playground. I had hand counted my first hundred thousand in cash, and that created a deeper hunger within me. I knew the streets didn't love me or hold no principles dear, so I lived according to the rules of savages. Eat or be ate!!

"I'm trinna take a small amount of money & turn it into a large amount of money." I announced driving around the city in my new X5 Jaguar.

"How large you talkin'?" Big Mike asked me.

"Large enough to break the scale!!"
Snowman getting murdered gave us a clear path at snatchin' certain neighborhoods, and I was trying to really capitalize off it.

Michael Belvins aka "Big Mike" was my right-hand man, and our bond had been battle tested a million times over the years. We had been mobbin' together since the sandbox, so I knew he had the heart to go against the gain with me.

"Let me play devil's advocate right quick. Once we're in power, why do we need Roller?" Big Mike questioned.

"We don't! He's just a piece on my chessboard. When we're in position, we can sacrifice em." I informed him. From the bottom to the top of the game, my lessons had been in depth. Nobody was safe from the vultures! Once they circled your block, bodies were destined to be found. Big Mike was a money getta, the best of the best if you asked me. What made him a real threat, was his ability to control the masses with his presence. Standing at 6'4" & 340 pounds, he was a giant to the average sized man. And his heart was even bigger!!

"I kinda figured that, but I just wanted to be sure. I'm not good with rockin' these niggas to sleep. I say blaze em all and let Allah sort em out! I respect your mind though." Big Mike reasoned.

"My mind is beyond these streets bro. We gotta start

thinking about movin' into different cities. Richmond is cool, but its other cities ready for the taking. I'm trying to see a million this year!"

"Then we gotta go harder! Loyalty put together a nice structure. Maybe we should just follow her blueprint and add our swag to it!"

"Not a bad idea my nigga, not a bad idea!"

(Miami)

"Hey!"

"What's up baby?" Teddy replied.

"I miss you! I know I haven't been visiting you much, but I've never stopped thinkin' about you." I confessed to him wholeheartedly.

"I think about you too. This prison shit ain't for me, and I think I found a way out." Teddy told me.

"How?"

"My roommate is down with the Trap Stars, and he's been telling me a lot of their business."

"You want me to holla at Ready?" I asked quickly.

"For what?"

"All he do is jack shit. My lil brother is on that shit full-fledged!"

"Naw shorty, I'm on some whole other shit." He said. Teddy had been my boyfriend for 4 years, and then he got incarcerated for a drug distribution case. I always thought he was gettin' it, but later I found out he was just a middleman. Big Mike from da bottom had put him on his feet, and that's how Teddy started flippin'. However, it wasn't long before he figured out that he wasn't a hustla. He fucked up Big Mike's work, and they put him in the hospital for 3 weeks. After that ass whippin', I thought Teddy was going legit but that wasn't the case. Instead, he hit the trap harder!! Eventually he ended up connecting with Roller, and that's when the money started flowin'. It wasn't long before Teddy was drapin' me in designer everything!! His dick was good, but the money was better.

"Like what?" I asked him hesitantly.

"Your cousin still a police detective?"

"Why? You bout to snitch nigga?" I responded in amazement.

"Shhhhh shorty. You gone fuck around & get me killed." Teddy announced looking around the visitation to make sure no one had heard me.

"Are you?"

"I wanna come home Miami. This shit ain't for me. So, yeah, I'll do whatever it takes to get back to you." He said leaning over & kissing me.

I knew the power of "Pussy", but I never knew it would make a man go against everything he believed in. Teddy was a good nigga, but he wasn't Roller. After 2 years of waiting, I had decided to move on. And who better to hook up with then my nigga's plug!

"You sure you wanna do that Teddy?" I asked massaging his face with my hands.

"Yeah. Set it up!"

(Ghost)

"How long have you been living in Richmond?" Brooklyn interrogated me.

"My entire life. I've never even contemplated moving nowhere else because this is my city!" I told her truthfully.

"I came out here to visit my aunt 7 years ago, and she got really sick during my stay. Long story short, I haven't been back to New York since."

"Do you ever miss it?"

"Of course, but my aunt is the only family I have left. I couldn't leave her for dead!"

Brooklyn had a certain way of looking right through me, and I

B.G. Meyers

loved how she made me feel. She was a breath of fresh air, and I needed that in my life. Things were always so gloomy for me. Even fuckin' Santana came with a price tag, and I wasn't sure if I was willing to pay it. I just wanted something real, something of substance.

"I understand that. That's how I feel about my friend Loyalty. She's all I have left, and I protect her with my heart & soul!"

"She sounds dope!"

"She is." I confirmed.

I watched as people walked pass us. I couldn't remember the last time I had sat on a park bench with someone & just talked. My life wasn't that simple. I dreamed of a regular life, but I had forfeited that at 15 when I caught my first body.

"When was your last relationship? Or should I say SERIOUS relationship?" She asked looking start into my eyes.

"I don't know. I'm not really the relationship type."

"Scared of love?"

"Could be." I said shrugging my shoulders.

I looked at Brooklyn for a long minute, trying to remember the last time I felt a sincere spark with a woman. I had sex a lot, but I never seemed to care about the woman. I needed to change that and stop neglecting love!

CHAPTER 6.
<u>LOYALTY</u>

"I can't believe these bitch ass niggas hatin' like that! Got the police comin' to yo house about some old shit. We won't even poppin' back then." Santana snapped.
We were at the bar drinking, and she was definitely feelin' it. The detectives had questioned me about a shooting from 2012. I honestly had nothing to do with it, but it seemed strange. My name was known in the streets for gettin' money, not being caught up in petty shit. Most of my beefs came from the trap. Niggas wanted my position, but I wasn't budging until my whole crew was straight.

"Somebody's trying to get me jammed, but it's cool." I said nonchalantly.

I was draped in a black bodysuit with some black & red Louis Vuitton heels on. My Loyalty medallion was flooded with vvs diamonds, and it made my outfit pop even more. When it came to being a bad bitch, I was in a class by myself. From my clothes to my cars, I made sure that all my stuff was A1. Damn, I missed Gunna! I wished he could see me now. How I had fucked the city up and kept the Trap Stars boomin'!! It took a lot, but I had done it. Now I just wanted a simple life. My own boutique, some properties somewhere else & a fresh start. Was I asking for too much?

"It ain't cool Loyalty. We all depend on you for something. It's time for us to step up & make sure you're good! Make sure you're protected from da wickedness of the world." Java announced.

"That's real shit!" Santana stamped.

"I know what y'all are saying, but the game is the game. Ain't no rules, no honor, no foundation. We have to establish those things amongst us." I fired back sippin' my patron.

Loyalty

B.G. Meyers

"Excuse me, are you Loyalty?" A dark-skinned brother asked.

He was neatly trimmed from his 360 waves to his beard. His outfit was designer, and his buss down Rolex was noticeable.

"Whose asking?" I replied not interested in having a conversation for real.

"I'm Bishop."

I had heard his name a few times, but I had never gotten a chance to put a face with the name. He was a up & coming dope boy with a lot of ambition, and he had big monkey nuts from what I heard. He was steppin' on all the local dealers. They were either coppin' from him or suffering the consequences. His method was very cocky, but I had seen it done before. The bully game wasn't the best way to control the market in my opinion.

"Nice to meet you Bishop, but I'm kinda in the middle of girl's night out." I told him sarcastically.

"I'm not trinna interrupt. I just wanted to introduce myself, because I'm sure we'll be rubbin' shoulders in the near future." He responded arrogantly.

"Rubbin' shoulders?" I repeated laughingly, then continued my thought...

"I'ma giant out here baby. You got a lot more growin' to do!"

"Uh huh." Santana added.

"I guess time will tell, huh?" Bishop said with murder in his eyes.

"I guess so." I fired back returning his murderous gaze.

Bishop finished off his glass of liquor in one gulp, and then he smiled at us as he made his exit.

"What was that all about?" Java asked.

"Dick swinging contest." I replied knowing how to deal with men like Bishop.

"Mmmm, I love those low swinging dicks." Santana announced.

We all burst into laughter & continued our girl's night out.

Loyalty

B.G. Meyers

(Bishop)

Yeah, Loyalty was everything I imaged she would be. Beautiful, witty, powerful & confident in her position. I had to respect her for puttin' in the pain she had put in, but she needed to acknowledge my presence out here. I was layin' shit down, and my name was ringin' at the highest levels. The streets feared murder when it had no intended direction, and I understood that to the fullest. I didn't care who I went at, I just wanted the end result to equal more riches for me & my team.

As I exited the bar, I looked back at Loyalty for a moment. She was laughing with her entourage, and deep down I felt clowned. She had dismissed me as if I was a nobody. Yeah, I'd show her. I climbed into my Yukon Denali & thought for a second. What could I do to make her uncomfortable? Then I reached into the backseat & grabbed my dracco. After inspecting it for a few minutes, I lowered the driver side window in my truck.

2 hours went by before Loyalty & her two friends exited the bar. I watched as they walked & talked about something without a care in the world. I lifted my gun & pointed it out the window. As I squeezed the trigger, me & Loyalty locked eyes.

(Loyalty)

"DUCK!!!" I yelled to my girls when the gunshots rang out.

BLLLLATTT! BLLAAAATTT!!!

I reached into my Prada purse & grabbed my 9mm glock. Without thinking, I pointed in the direction of Bishop's truck & fired. It seemed like his shots were everlasting, and they were making contact with almost every parked car in the parking lot.

BLAAAATT! BLLLAATT!! BLLLAAATTT!!!

I continued to shoot without aiming, hoping that one of my bullets would crash into Bishop's brain. No matter how it went, if I lived to give the order, he would be murdered on sight!! I ducked down behind a tan caravan and waited for some type of motion. Car tires were screeching, and then complete silence fell over the parking lot.

"Santana!" I called out for her.

"Yeah girl." She answered sounding panicked.

"You okay."

"Yeah!"

"Java." I called out still hiding.

No answer followed. Which made me raise my voice.

"JAVA!!" I yelled.

When she didn't answer my second call, I peeked around the back of the van. I saw her still body lying on the ground. Blood was everywhere, and she didn't appear to be breathing.

"Oh, SHIT!!" I screamed rushing to her rescue.

"OH MY GOD, JAVA, WAKE UP!! WAKE UP!!" Santana cried shaking her little cousin.

I couldn't believe what just happened. Bishop had shot & killed one of my friends because I didn't wanna acknowledge him. Now he would have to die early, and Ghost would be sure of it. Mo' money, mo' murder over politics!!

CHAPTER 7.
<u>N A S A</u>

"You nervous my nigga?" Teddy asked me.

"Yeah. I've never been involved in something like this before. You know how the old saying goes"...

"Never rat out your friends!"

"Exactly. Now here I am ready to give up da whole gang. This shit don't feel right. I feel like less than a man." I confessed.

"Why? Because you're taking your freedom back. That bitch ain't thinkin' bout you, my nigga. She out there doin' it big, and you're in here eating noodles every night. Man, up nigga, and go home to your family!" Teddy stressed knowing he was about to do the same.

"I hear you bro." I replied.

This meeting with Detective Martin was my ticket back to the city. I knew I would be a target once I crossed Loyalty, but I was willin' to take my chances. Besides, none of the Trap Stars were holding me down. That shit wasn't family!

I pressed the intercom button in my cell and told the booth officer I was ready to go to my meeting. Once the cell door came open, I knew shit was real!

"Do what you gotta do my nigga!" Teddy encouraged me.

(Roller)

"Ohhh, my ggod, fuck me baby, fuck me good!" Miami moaned.

B.G. Meyers

I had been sexin' her for the last 10 minutes, and I couldn't seem to get enough of her.

"Turn over." I told her.

I watched as she flipped over & put ass in the air. She immediately braced herself, looking back at me with a seductive look on her face. I loved the way her ass spreaded when she bent it over for me. I positioned myself directly behind her, then pushed my dick into her pussy as hard as I could.

"Ooouuu, ffucckkkk, I love that shit, looove it!" She moaned throwing her ass back at me.

I began to pound her from the back, wanting her to feel every inch of my manhood. The sounds of her wetness only motivated me more. Faster & deeper until I was on the verge of cumming.

"I'm bout to buss in you bae. Take it, take it allll!" I groaned & grunted as I released my load inside of her.

Once we both we finished climaxing, we fell on the bed side by side.

"Damn, you got a missile. I mean the best I've ever had!" I stated wholeheartedly.

"I feel the same way. I wished I would've met you first." Miami said.

"What you mean?" I asked irritated by her statement.

"I feel a little guilty sometimes, because Teddy was your friend."

"That nigga was a worker. Our relationship was about money. You on the other hand, should be showin' him some type of loyalty." I informed her based on what I knew regarding their bond.

"He ain't my type of nigga. I fuck wit gangstas, not rats!" She announced.

"Teddy's a rat?" I interrogated her for my protection.

"I went to see him Saturday, and he said his roommate is a Trap Star. Must be somebody important, because he's telling Teddy all their business & he's ready to use it to get out." Miami revealed.

"What?! That's crazy! I never pent brah to be that

type of nigga. Plus, he ain't buried, he doin' a skid bid."

"I don't know. I just wanna be wit you. I love how you fuck me Roller." She said grabbing my dick & stroking it back to life.

Teddy was wildin'! I knew he was doing a bid for Loyalty's crew, but I ain't think he would go this far. Snitching was a major offense in the streets, and he had to be desperate to even consider it. I knew this information would gain me favor with Loyalty, so I planned on using it to my advantage.

"Do that thing I like with your tongue." I told Miami.

"Okay baby."

(Bishop)

With so many rules in the streets, it's hard to pick the right ones to abide by. My mentor was a certified jack boy name "C-Rock", and he had given me the game from a different perspective. His ideology was simply, only the strong survived. In time I started to see life through those same eyes. Make money or take money! So, when it was my turn to lead, I gave those same teachings to my young niggas.

"What's up big bruh?" Gangland asked when I entered the trap house.

"Nothin'. Just had to put on for us one time." I replied.

"Fo sho!"

"What's the traffic like tonight?" I asked curiously.

"Shit movin' bruh. I'm thinkin' about doin' a special." Sean explained.

"What kind of special?" I asked.

"I haven't figured it out yet. They say them niggas uptown jumpin' wit da food. Joe Joe been keepin' me sharp." Sean said looking straight at me.

"If they're really pipin', go get that! Nobody is safe

B.G. Meyers

my nigga, NOBODY!!!"

It was time to turn up in the city, and I had already set the bar high. Loyalty was untouchable to most people, but to me she was just a pretty female. I couldn't & wouldn't sleep on her though because she hadn't made it this long in the game by being weak or dumb. Our little encounter tonight definitely put me on her radar, and I was happy about it. You couldn't become a legend without doing legendary shit! I knew her playbook, so that put me ahead of the game. Her next move would be to send Ghost to step on me, but I would be ready for him. Waiting patiently for him to come huntin', praying that he made a mistake along the way. Murder would be my claim to fame!

"We bout to gear up now!" Gangland announced puttin' on his robbery attire.

"Has anybody talked to my uncle?" I inquired.

"Naw, he hasn't called in a few days." Sean said. My uncle "Teddy" had been like a father to me over the years, that was until he got locked up! I still looked up to him, and I sent him money every chance I got. Lately, he had been sounding down, almost like was depressed about something. I couldn't comfort him though because I'd never been on the inside before. I didn't know what it was like or how it felt to be captured. Caged like a wild animal, and I swore I would never fall victim to that reality. I would commit suicide first! That's why I named my crew "Death B4." Most people assumed it meant Death B4 Dishonor, but that wasn't true. I believed if we killed the right people, then we would live forever!!!

CHAPTER 8.
ROLLER

"What's good, beautiful?" I greeted Loyalty as she walked up on the porch of my trap house.

"What you on my nigga?" Loyalty responded with a grim look in her eyes.

Ghost stood at the bottom of the steps, and neither of them seemed to be in a good mood. I was trying to gain favor & position with this meeting, but it didn't seem to be going how I imagined.

"Everything okay?" I asked Loyalty.

"Naw, everything isn't okay. Look, you told me to meet up with you it was urgent. What's going on?"

"You got a rat in your camp." I announced.

"Who?" She questioned with a blank stare.

"Teddy."

"Never heard of him."

"He's not directly associated with the Trap Stars, but he's roommates with one of your top movers. Dude is talkin' too much, and we both know loose lips sink ships!" I said convincingly.

"You still ain't dropped a name Roller." Loyalty pointed out.

"NASA is his roommate." I revealed.

"Shit!" Ghost exclaimed.

"How sure are you?" Loyalty asked.

"100%. I'm fuckin' Teddy's girl. She just went to visit him last weekend, and he told her his plan. He gone turn state evidence in exchange for a pass on the rest of his time."

"Good lookin' my nigga!" She responded snappin' her fingers.

Loyalty

B.G. Meyers

Ghost immediately came up the stairs & began to pat me down for a wire. I wasn't feeling that at all, and my facial expression showed it.

"What da fuck?" I blurted out.

"Can't be too careful now a days." Loyalty said shrugging her shoulders.

(Ghost)

Once we were in the car, I looked over at Loyalty. For the first time in a long time, she looked stressed! I didn't know how this would play out for us, but I wasn't gonna abandon her now.

"How we gone handle this?" I asked.

"I don't know honestly. NASA always came across as a solid nigga, but them prison walls bring out different sides of people." Loyalty reasoned.

"We could pay his mother a visit." I offered.

"That'll make it worse. We gotta find a way to get to him on the inside."

"Hakeem is lock up there. 5 thousand will go a long way."

"Send 10 to be sure it's quiet." She ordered without much thought.

We rode the rest of the ride in silence. My thoughts were all over the place. Murder had been my contribution to the family, and I never once tried to color outside of those lines. Body after body had given my position worth, but now we were talking about governmental officials. This was bigger than the streets. Hakeem would handle our inside leak, but that was one of many problems that were occurring. Bishop had to be hit for transgressing against the family. His name was buzzin' right now, and Death B4 had the street's attention. I'd climinate him sooner than later, because problems weren't meant to linger. A problem was like a life-threatening cancer, if you didn't kill it at the root, it would grow until it killed you!

I circled the block once when I got to Loyalty's house. I wanted to make no one was tailing us or staked out around her crib. I pulled into a parking space and unlocked her door from the door panel on my side.

"Goodnight." She said as she climbed outta my car.

"Goodnight." I responded.

I waited until she was inside her house before I pulled out into traffic. I had murder on my mind. I just didn't know where I would start.

(NASA)

As I headed to the interview room to meet with Detective Martin, it seemed like the longest walk ever! My mind was racing with so many thoughts, and I wasn't sure if I could actually go through with it. For some reason Teddy was pushing me, but so many things about him really didn't make sense to me. First, he told me that he had only been in Virginia for a few days before he got arrested, but then Miami came to visit him. I knew Miami well. She didn't have the best reputation in Richmond. She was known as a clout chaser, and only niggas that didn't know were fuckin' wit her. Then he kept asking me all these questions about the Trap Stars. I didn't understand it, and I couldn't put my finger on it either.

I prayed that the decision I made wasn't the wrong one, because I knew there could be major consequences for my disloyalty. But how were the Trap Stars being loyal to me? I wasn't living good on the inside; I was barely making it. After all the drugs I sold for them, you would think I was up! I just wanted to be free again. To be with my son. I had missed the important parts of his beginning, and not one of my niggas had been there for him. I had to find my own way

B.G. Meyers

out, and this was the quickest way to freedom. I entered the interview room convinced I would give them what I had to for them to release me.

"Mr. Evans, I'm glad you decided to take me up on my offer." Detective Martin said with a cheesy grin on his face.

"Yeah, being free is more important to me." I replied not feeling confident in what I was doing.

"So, let's get to the point of this meeting." The Detective said turning on a tape recorder.

"Alright."

"What do you know about Gregory Bateman's death?"

"Everything! I was there when it happened. Sitting in my car smoking a blunt when he was shot & killed. I even know where the murder weapon is stashed." I blurted out to the Detective.

"Mr. Wagner told us you would be beneficial." Detective Martin stated.

Teddy Wagner had been playing me this whole time. I didn't understand it though. After his visit with Miami, he told me that he was considering doing the same thing to his crew back home. Me & him had had a heart to heart that night, and that's what pushed me to agree to these terms.

"Who killed Gregory Bateman?" The Detective asked impatiently.

"Lana Jackson."

TO BE CONTINUED!!!!!

Made in the USA
Middletown, DE
24 September 2023

39101618R00024